Sarah
the Sunday
Fairy

For Sara O'Connor,
who has helped the
fairies on countless occasions!

Special thanks to
Narinder Dhami

ISBN-10: 0-545-06762-6
ISBN-13: 978-0-545-06762-1

12 11 10 9 8 7 6 5 4 3   9 10 11 12 13/0

Printed in the U.S.A.

First Scholastic Printing, August 2008

Sarah
the Sunday
Fairy

by Daisy Meadows

SCHOLASTIC INC.

New York   Toronto   London   Auckland   Sydney

Mexico City   New Delhi   Hong Kong   Buenos Aires

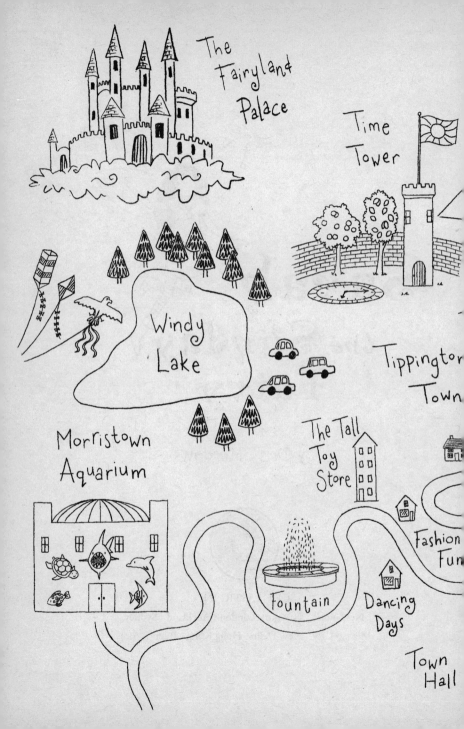

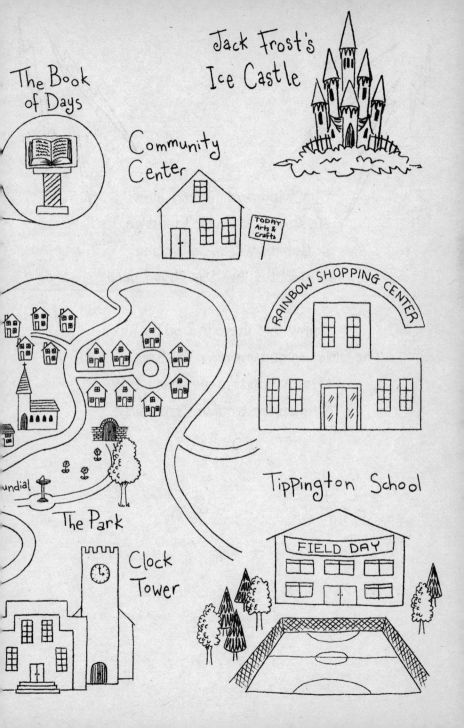

Jack Frost's
Ice Castle

The Book
of Days

Community
Center

TODAY
Arts &
Crafts

RAINBOW SHOPPING CENTER

Tippington School

FIELD DAY

undial

The Park

Clock
Tower

Icy wind now fiercely blow!
To the Time Tower I must go.
Goblins will all follow me
And steal the Fun Day Flags I need.

I know that there will be no fun,
For fairies or humans once the flags are gone.
Storm winds, take me where I say.
My plan for trouble starts today!

Contents

Gobbling Goblin   1

A Second Stowaway   15

Kirsty's Big Idea   29

A Frosty Fake   39

The Real Jack Frost   47

A Perfect Picnic   55

Gobbling Goblin

"I can't believe it's Sunday already!"
Kirsty Tate said, glancing at her best
friend, Rachel Walker. They were in the
Walkers' kitchen, wrapping sandwiches
in plastic bags. "My mom and dad are
coming to pick me up tonight," Kirsty
added. "This week has gone so quickly!"

"Yes, it has," Rachel agreed. "That's

because we've been busy looking for the fairies' Fun Day Flags!"

Just then, Mr. Walker hurried in, carrying a large straw picnic basket. Rachel stopped talking immediately and grinned at Kirsty. Nobody else knew that the two girls had a magical secret: they were friends with the fairies!

For the last week, the two girls had been trying to find the missing Fun Day Flags and return them to the seven Fun Day Fairies. The flags were very important. The fairies used the magic in the flags to make every day of the week fun.

The trouble had started when naughty Jack Frost and his goblins stole the flags. When the flags' special magic made the goblins only want to have fun, Jack Frost became so annoyed that he cast a spell that sent the flags whirling into the human world. But his mischievous goblins had missed having fun so much that they escaped into the human world to try to get the flags back. Of course, Jack Frost did not know about the goblins' plan.

"Let's hurry up and pack the food, girls," said Mr. Walker, putting the picnic basket on the table. "We want to get an early start so we can make the most of this sunny weather."

"It was a wonderful idea to have a picnic at Windy Lake, Dad," Rachel said, as she popped a plastic container of potato salad into the basket.

"And all this food looks delicious," Kirsty added, looking at a large peach pie.

"Put the pie and sandwiches in last, or they'll get squished," Mr. Walker suggested as the girls added bottles of water to the basket. "Will you finish packing while I get the car out of the garage?"

Kirsty and Rachel nodded.

"We only have Sarah the Sunday Fairy's flag left to find now," Rachel said, when Mr. Walker had gone.

"Yes, but this is the last flag. So the goblins will be even more determined to find it first," Kirsty pointed out.

Rachel put a picnic blanket on top of the food and closed the basket as Mrs. Walker came in.

"That looks heavy, Rachel," she said. "Leave it for your dad to carry. I'm just going to bring Buttons in from the backyard."

Rachel and Kirsty ran upstairs to get their jackets. As they came downstairs, Mr. Walker staggered out of the kitchen. He was carrying the picnic basket with both hands.

"This basket weighs a ton!" he groaned. "Did you pack a peach pie for each of us, girls?"

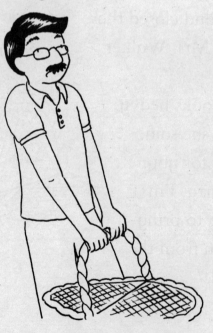

Kirsty and Rachel laughed as Mrs. Walker and Buttons joined them. The shaggy dog sniffed the air and then launched himself at the picnic basket, barking excitedly.

"Calm down, Buttons!" Rachel said, pulling him back. "I put some biscuits in for you, but you have to wait until we get to Windy Lake."

They all climbed into the car and set off. Buttons woofed eagerly at the picnic basket throughout their trip.

"It's a good thing Windy Lake isn't very far away," Rachel said, grinning. After a short drive, Mr. Walker turned off the main road onto a narrow, bumpy path.

As they reached the end of the path, Kirsty gasped with delight. "Oh, this is perfect!" she cried.

In front of them was a large, shimmering lake, surrounded by green woods. A few other people were picnicking, walking their dogs, and feeding the ducks on the lake. Even though the area was beautiful, the girls could see that the people weren't having much fun.

"We need to find the Sunday flag," Rachel whispered, "so the fairies can put the fun back into Sunday."

Kirsty nodded as Mr. Walker parked the car and they all climbed out.

"That's a good spot for a picnic," said Rachel's mom, pointing to a shady tree near the water's edge. They headed over to the tree, with Buttons pulling frantically at his leash and Mr. Walker struggling with the picnic basket.

"I think Buttons needs a walk to calm him down," Mr. Walker suggested, putting the basket down with a sigh of relief. "Why don't you girls unpack the food while we take him for a quick run?"

"Good idea," said Mrs. Walker, taking the leash from Rachel.

Buttons trotted reluctantly after Mr. and Mrs. Walker. He glanced back at the picnic basket every so often.

"I wonder what's wrong with Buttons," Rachel said. "I've never seen him act like that before —" Suddenly, she

stopped and frowned. "What's that rustling noise?"

Kirsty pointed at the picnic basket. "I think it's coming from in there," she whispered.

"It might be Sarah the Sunday Fairy!" Rachel said, excitedly, carefully lifting the lid of the basket.

She and Kirsty peeked inside, and both cried out in surprise. There sat a big green goblin holding a sandwich in his hands. His mouth was wide open, and he was about to take a huge bite!

A Second Stowaway

"That's my turkey sandwich!" Rachel gasped, grabbing the sandwich out of the goblin's hand just in time.

As his teeth crunched down on a mouthful of air, the goblin shot a furious glance at Rachel. "Give that back!" he demanded in a gruff voice.

"No, it's not yours!" Rachel replied, hiding the sandwich behind her back.

"What are you doing in our picnic basket, anyway?" asked Kirsty.

"I'm not going to tell you!" the goblin muttered.

"Why not?" asked Rachel.

"Because I'm not going to tell you anything," the goblin said firmly. "I'm especially not going to tell you that we're looking for the Sunday Fun Flag, because you're not allowed to know about that!" Then he frowned and clapped a hand over his mouth.

"Too late!" Rachel said cheerfully. "You just told us."

Scowling, the goblin grabbed a chocolate chip cookie, jumped out of the basket, and scurried into the trees.

"I wonder if that means the Sunday flag is around here somewhere," Kirsty said thoughtfully.

Meanwhile, Rachel was looking in the basket. "Where is the picnic blanket?" she asked. "The goblin must have taken it out to make room for himself!"

"No wonder Buttons was so excited," Kirsty said. "He must have smelled the goblin inside the basket."

"I hope the goblin hasn't eaten a lot of food!" Rachel said, taking out the wrapped sandwiches and checking them. "How will we explain that to Mom and Dad?"

The girls unpacked the basket, but none of the food seemed to be missing except the one chocolate chip cookie the goblin had stolen.

"Looks like we found him just in time," Kirsty laughed. Then suddenly she clutched Rachel's arm. "Look!" she gasped. "I can see magic sparkles!"

Rachel's heart began to pound. She could see dazzling silver sparkles drifting up from behind an apple in the corner of the basket, too!

Carefully, Kirsty moved the apple aside. Behind it sat an untidy little fairy, her long black hair tangled and messy. The fairy saw the girls looking down at

her and waved at them with her wand. Then she jumped to her feet, shook out her short yellow dress, and smoothed her shiny hair.

"Hello, girls!" she called. "It's me, Sarah the Sunday Fairy. Thanks for getting rid of the goblin. I was getting really squished in that corner!"

"Hello, Sarah," Rachel said happily as the fairy stretched her crumpled wings and fluttered out of the basket. "We

think your flag might be close by. Why else would the goblin be here?"

Sarah nodded eagerly. "Yes, you're right," she said. "The Book of Days gave us a clue."

In Fairyland, Francis the frog checked the Book of Days every morning. Francis was the Fairyland Royal Time Guard, and it was his job to fly the correct day's flag at the top of the Time Tower in the palace gardens. When the sun struck the flag, the Fun Day Fairy in charge of that day of the week would recharge her wand in its magic rays. But since the flags had gone missing, poems that gave clues to the flags' whereabouts now appeared in the Book of Days.

Sarah recited the newest poem:

"The Sunday flag likes picnic fun.
You're sure to find it in the sun.
Jack Frost's goblins want it, too,
So getting it first is up to you!"

"I think the goblins must have been hiding somewhere in the courtyard when Francis read the poem out loud, so they overheard it," Sarah explained. "That's  why one of them hid in your picnic basket!"

"We'll just have to make sure we find the flag first," Kirsty said. Sarah nodded. "We must be careful, though," she added. "I'm sure there are a lot more goblins around. After all, this is their last chance to get a Fun Day Flag!"

Woof! came a happy bark from behind them.

Rachel glanced around to see her mom, dad, and Buttons coming toward them. "Sarah, you'd better hide," she whispered.

Quickly, Sarah zoomed over to Kirsty and hid in her pocket.

"I think Buttons has worked off some of his extra energy!" Mrs. Walker laughed as they joined the girls.

"We saw a man flying a fantastic kite on the other side of the lake," Mr. Walker added. "It was a big red dragon with a long blue tail. Keep an eye out for it."

Rachel's mom gave the girls a puzzled look. "Where's the blanket, Rachel?" she asked.

"Oh, um, I must have forgotten to put it in the basket," Rachel said quickly. She couldn't tell her mom that a goblin probably threw it out!

"Don't worry," said Mrs. Walker. "There's a blanket in the car. I left it by the window in the backseat after the Craft Fair on Wednesday. Will you get

it?" She handed Rachel the keys and the
girls headed to the car.

As they came within sight of it, Rachel
blinked. She couldn't
believe her eyes! It looked
like someone was
standing on the roof.

Suddenly, Rachel
realized what it
was. "There's
a goblin on
the roof of the
car!" she exclaimed
in surprise.

"And there are two
of them standing on the
trunk," Kirsty added.

"And another two on the hood!"
whispered Sarah.

The goblins were staring into the Walkers' car. As Sarah and the girls got closer, they saw that there were two more goblins. One was standing on the other's shoulders, so he could look in through a side window.

"That makes seven goblins altogether," Rachel said, sounding anxious.

"What are they looking at?" Kirsty asked.

The girls crept up quietly behind the goblins to find out.

"Let me have a look!" complained the goblin who was holding the other one on his shoulders. "It's my turn now!"

Rachel stepped forward very carefully, so the goblins didn't hear her. She looked into the car herself. She could see the striped blanket her mother had mentioned lying by the back windshield, and poking out from underneath it was some silver fabric with a glittering sun pattern on it.

"Oh!" Rachel whispered. "I think the Sunday flag is inside our car!"

Kirsty's Big Idea

Sarah and Kirsty looked where Rachel was pointing. Then they all hurried to hide behind a big oak tree before the goblins noticed them.

"It *is* my flag!" Sarah exclaimed.

"But the goblins know just where it is," Kirsty said. "What are we going to do?"

"Well, the flag's safe inside the car,"

Rachel said. "But how are we
going to get it out?"

"We'll have to get the
goblins away from
the car," Kirsty
said thoughtfully.
"But how?"

"Look!" one of the
goblins shouted.

The girls peeked
around the tree to
see what was
happening. The
goblin standing on
the car roof was
pointing up at the sky.
He looked excited.

"What's he pointing at?"
asked Kirsty.

She and Rachel stared across the lake. In the distance, they could see a red-and-blue kite, shaped like a dragon, swooping and soaring on the breeze. "It's the kite Dad was talking about," Rachel whispered. "I can see a kite shaped like a dragon!" the goblin shouted gleefully. "But none of you can! Ha, ha, ha!" The other goblins scowled. "I want to see it!" one moaned.

"Let me look at it!" cried another.

Pushing and shoving, the other six
goblins climbed onto the roof of the car
to see the kite for themselves.

"We could try to get the flag while
they're watching the kite. . . ." Rachel
suggested.

But then the goblins gave a loud groan.

"The pretty kite went behind that big
tree," one of them grumbled, sliding
down from the roof.

"We can't waste any more time,"
another goblin pointed out. "How are
we going to get the flag out of
this car?"

"That kite gave me an idea!" Kirsty
whispered, her
face glowing
with excitement.
"Sarah, could you
use your magic to
make a wonderful
kite? One that
would distract the
goblins?"

Sarah grinned.
"What a great
idea!" she said and
fluttered up into the
air, waving her wand.

There was a burst of magic sparkles above the girls' heads, and a golden string appeared in Kirsty's hand. The girls looked up. High in the sky, at the end of the string, was a beautiful golden kite shaped like a phoenix. It had a long rainbow-colored tail that swished back and forth as the kite swooped this way and that.

Kirsty stepped out from behind the car so that the goblins could see the kite. "This kite is so much fun!" she said loudly, making the kite swoop from side to side. "I'm having a wonderful time!"

The goblins stared at the kite, their eyes wide. Soon, they forgot all about the flag and began to scamper away from the car and toward Kirsty.

"Can I try it?" the biggest goblin asked.

"No, me first!" another shouted, pushing the first goblin out of the way.

"You can all have a turn," said Kirsty, handing the string out to the nearest goblin.

Meanwhile, Sarah and Rachel tiptoed over to the Walkers' car. Her heart thumping, Rachel quietly unlocked the door, reached in, and grabbed the flag. She tried to shut the door quietly, but one of the goblins heard the noise and looked around.

"Hey!" he shrieked. "They're taking the flag!"

The goblin holding the kite string let go, and all seven goblins charged back to the car. Anxiously, Kirsty followed them as they surrounded Sarah and Rachel.

"Give that to me!" one of the goblins snapped. He tried to grab the flag, but Rachel held it up out of his reach.

"Rachel, look out!" Kirsty cried, as she saw another of the goblins scrambling onto the roof of the car.

But she was too late. The goblin reached down and grabbed the flag right out of Rachel's hand!

A Frosty Fake

"I've got the flag!" the goblin cackled
with glee. Then he jumped down from
the car and ran off into the woods. The
others followed him.

"After them!" Rachel gasped.

The girls chased the goblins into the
woods with Sarah zooming right next to
them. But the goblins were fast runners.

Rachel and Kirsty were soon out of
breath, especially since the goblins kept
dodging in and out of the trees.

"We have to make them stop." Kirsty
panted. "But how?"

"I know what would slow them
down," Rachel said breathlessly. "Jack
Frost!"

Kirsty and Sarah looked confused.

"The goblins aren't supposed to be looking for the flags, are they?" Rachel pointed out. "So they would be terrified if an angry Jack Frost appeared — or if they saw something that they thought was Jack Frost!"

Sarah grinned. "I can't make a Jack Frost look-alike appear out of thin air," she said, "but I can make something else look like Jack Frost."

Sarah pointed her wand at an old tree stump a little further ahead of the goblins. A stream of silver sparkles shot from the wand and surrounded the

stump. It immediately seemed to change
shape, becoming a tall, icy-looking
figure with a nasty frown.

The goblin at the front of the crowd
skidded to a halt. "It's Jack Frost!" he
gasped.

All the other goblins bumped into the
back of him, then huddled together
looking terrified.

"Hello, master," one goblin muttered
nervously. "How, um, nice to see you."

"It wasn't my fault," another whined.
"It was their idea to look for the flag."

The goblin holding the flag looked the
most scared of all. He hurried forward
and bowed to the tree stump. "The flag
is a special present for you, master," he
said, holding it out.

Then he frowned
and looked more
closely at the tree
stump. He gave it a
hard poke, and all
the goblins gasped.

"It's not Jack
Frost!" the goblin
shouted, looking
very relieved. "It's
just an old tree
stump!"

The other goblins seemed puzzled, but
then one of them spotted Sarah and the
girls just behind them.

"It was fairy magic!" he shouted,
pointing at them.

"Ha!" yelled the goblin with the flag.
"You didn't fool us!"

Sarah, Rachel, and Kirsty glanced at
each other in dismay. But at that
moment, a cold wind swirled out of
nowhere, and an icy figure appeared
behind the goblins.

"It's Jack Frost!" Kirsty cried. "He's
behind you."

"I told you, you can't fool us that
easily," insisted the goblin with the flag.

Jack Frost crossed his arms behind the
gloating goblins. He looked furious.
"GIVE ME THAT FLAG!" he bellowed.

The Real Jack Frost

Unable to believe their ears, the goblins spun around to face Jack Frost.

"GIVE ME THAT FLAG!" Jack Frost roared again. And he waved his wand, shooting icy lightning bolts all around the clearing.

Pale with fright, the goblins scattered, diving behind rocks and tree trunks.

The goblin holding the flag was so scared that he dropped it on the ground in front of Jack Frost, and then jumped into the middle of a bush.

Sarah, Rachel, and Kirsty also dashed behind a tree, dodging flying lightning bolts all the way.

"I've had enough of this!" Jack Frost
snapped, picking up the flag. "I've been
sitting in my castle, calling for my
slippers, but nobody brought them!
And why?" He shook the flag. "Because
all my goblins ran off to search for this
silly flag!"

He quickly rounded up his goblins. They stood very sheepishly in front of him.

"Please, sir," the biggest goblin said. "Now that we have the flag, we can all go back to the ice castle, and we'll bring you your slippers whenever you want!"

Sarah looked discouraged. "We can't let Jack Frost take the flag back to his ice castle," she said anxiously. "We have to stop him."

Rachel and Kirsty exchanged a determined look, and then stepped bravely from behind the tree. Their knees shook as Jack Frost glared at them.

"If you take the flag back to your castle, the goblins will have so much fun they'll start playing pranks again," Rachel told Jack Frost. "Have you

forgotten about that trick they played, when the bucket of water fell on your head?"

Jack Frost frowned.

"And when you ask for your slippers, the goblins will probably fill them with mud as a joke!" Kirsty added. "Are you sure you want the flag?"

Jack Frost looked furious but thoughtful. He was clearly thinking about what the girls had said.

Rachel and Kirsty waited, trying not to shiver in the freezing air. What would Jack Frost decide?

A Perfect Picnic

Suddenly, Jack Frost stepped forward.
"Take the flag!" he snapped, handing it
to Rachel. "But the fairies must promise
to keep the Fun Day Flags safe, and
never ever let the goblins touch them
again!" He glared at Sarah. "Do you
promise?" he demanded.

Sarah grinned. "I promise," she replied firmly.

Jack Frost nodded and turned to his troop of goblins. "Quick, march!" he shouted.

Sarah, Kirsty, and Rachel couldn't help smiling as the goblins trudged after Jack Frost, looking extremely disappointed.

"Thank you, girls." Sarah laughed. "Now I have my precious flag back!" She waved her wand over it and the flag immediately shrank down to its Fairyland size.

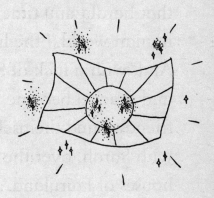

"What happened to the magic kite?" asked Kirsty, staring up into the air.

"It dissolved magically in the breeze," Sarah explained with a smile. "And now, why don't you come back to Fairyland with me to give everyone the good news?"

"We'd love to," Rachel replied. "But my parents will start wondering where we are soon."

"Don't worry, I can send you back so that hardly any time has passed in the human world," the little fairy promised. And, with a flick of Sarah's wand, Kirsty and Rachel became fairies again. The friends found themselves zooming along with Sarah, over the pretty toadstool houses of Fairyland.

Looking down, the girls could see lots of fairies in the palace gardens.

"What's happening?" Rachel asked
curiously.

"They're having a picnic!" Sarah
giggled.

As they flew closer to the ground,
Kirsty and Rachel could see that the
fairies, including King Oberon and
Queen Titania, were sitting in the Time
Tower courtyard on soft blankets spun
from threads of silvery cobwebs. The

fairies were surrounded by golden plates
piled with sandwiches, cakes, and
cookies. But the girls could see
that nobody was having
much fun.

"Look!" cried Francis
the frog, hurrying
forward with the Book
of Days in his arms.
"It's Sarah, Rachel, and
Kirsty. They have the
Sunday Fun Flag!"

The fairies clapped
joyfully as Sarah and the girls fluttered
to the ground.

"Welcome, Rachel and Kirsty,"
Queen Titania said sweetly. "Once
again, we cannot thank you enough for
all your help!"

"And now Sarah must recharge her wand with Fun Day magic," King Oberon added, "or Sunday will be over and we won't have had any fun at all!"

Everyone watched as Sarah ran over to stand at the center of the giant clock in the middle of the courtyard. Meanwhile, Francis hopped quickly inside the Time Tower. A moment later everyone cheered as he hauled the Sunday flag to the top of the flagpole.

"Here comes the Fun Day magic!" Kirsty said to Rachel when the sun's rays struck the flag.

Sarah held up her wand. As the magical rays streamed down toward her, the wand began to fizz with silver sparkles. "Now Sundays can be fun again!" Sarah cried.

She pointed her wand at the courtyard and sent a sparkling cloud of Fun Day magic showering over the whole picnic.

Suddenly, shiny paper chains
and glittery balloons
decorated the trees, and a huge
plate of fairy cakes with
pink, blue, yellow, and
green icing appeared in
a flash of magic.
"Thanks to you,
girls, we have all
our Fun Day Flags
again," Queen
Titania said as the
seven Fun Day
Fairies gathered
around her.
"And the Book of Days
is back to normal, too,"
declared Francis happily as he
hurried out of the Time Tower.

"You must join our picnic," King Oberon added.

"Thank you," Rachel said gratefully. "But we have our own picnic to eat back at Windy Lake. We don't want to spoil our appetites."

King Oberon smiled. "Oh, but think how small one of our fairy cakes will be when you're human-sized again!" he pointed out.

The girls laughed and took a fairy cake each. As they ate, they watched the fairies dancing. They even got to join in playing party games. Everyone was having so much fun that Kirsty and

Rachel were sorry when it was time to leave.

"Sarah will go with you to the human world to put some Fun Day magic back into Sunday," Queen Titania told them. "And look out for a special fairy surprise back at the lake!"

"Thank you again, my dears," said King Oberon. "And good-bye for now."

All the fairies clustered around Kirsty and Rachel. "Good-bye, and thank you!" they cried.

Then Sarah waved her wand, and she, Kirsty, and Rachel left for Windy Lake in a mist of magic sparkles.

"Let's find the blanket, Rachel," said Kirsty, as they arrived back at the Walkers' car.

"I have some Fun Day magic work to do," said Sarah, spinning happily in the air. "Good-bye, Kirsty and Rachel."

The two friends waved as the tiny fairy fluttered away. Then they collected the picnic blanket from the car and hurried back to the lake.

As the girls neared their picnic spot, Buttons rushed up to meet them, followed by Rachel's dad.

"Girls," Mr. Walker called breathlessly, "look what just landed near us!" He held out two beautiful kites. One was pink, the other yellow, and they glittered in the sun, just like the Fun Day Flags. Both the kites had long, rainbow-colored tails.

"Read the messages on them," Mr. Walker insisted.

The girls saw that both kites had messages tied to their tails. The messages read:

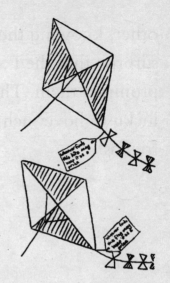

Whoever finds this kite
may keep it as a prize.
We hope it brings delight,
swooping through the skies!

"Isn't that lucky?" Rachel's dad smiled at them. "You can each have a kite! Do you want to try them out now?"

Rachel and Kirsty grinned at each

other, knowing that this must be the surprise that the Fairy Queen had promised them. They both felt very lucky to have such wonderful fairy friends!

Special Edition

Rachel and Kirsty have rescued all of
the Fun Day Flags, but they still have lots
of fairy adventures to come! Check out
this special sneak peek of

Stella
the Star
Fairy!

Darkness Falls

Mrs. Tate popped her head around
the door. "Are you ready, girls?" she
asked. "It's time to leave for the
Christmas Fair."

"Coming, Mom," Kirsty said,
jumping up.

"I'm really glad I could come and
visit," said Rachel Walker, as she

followed her best friend into the hall to get their coats. Rachel was visiting over Christmas break. Her parents were picking her up on Christmas Eve.

"Me, too," Kirsty replied. "You're going to love the fair. And who knows, maybe we'll see a Christmas fairy!"

Rachel and Kirsty thought they were the luckiest girls in the world, because they had become friends with the fairies! Whenever the fairies were in trouble, they asked the girls for help.

"I forgot to tell you!" Kirsty said, pulling on her boots. "Every year, someone from my school is chosen to be the fair's Christmas King or Queen. This year, it's my friend Molly."

"Wow!" said Rachel, smiling. "I'd love to be Christmas Queen!"